JOURNEY 5

A NOVELLA

E.L. BEAN

INDIES UNITED PUBLISHING HOUSE, LLC

INDIES UNITED PUBLISHING HOUSE, LLC
P.O. BOX 3071
QUINCY, IL 62305-3071
www.indiesunited.net

Dedicated to all those lost souls who
try to find their way…

PROLOGUE

There are two realities in a man's life. The first is being dead in heaven without being able to enjoy it. The second is living in hell without being able to die. A hell, where even the sound of the word sends shivers down your spine. An endless waterfall that you cannot touch while thirsty, a warm, cozy bed, where you cannot lay while exhausted. It's like praying to die, but death turns its back each time you attempt to reach him.

"The fear of death follows from the fear of life," Mark Twain once wrote, and as I was checking through my mailbox on that cold October afternoon, I found something strange inside. A big, heavy envelope. A book, perhaps? I read the name on the side. It was from my good friend Luck, whom I haven't seen in ages. She was too busy with her murder cases as homicide detective, and I was too busy finding excuses to avoid social interaction.

A letter from her made me curious. I didn't pay attention to the rest of the letters that were in my mailbox. With quick steps, I walked back to the apartment, eager to open the package. Anxiously, I sat at my desk, took a deep breath, and looked outside my window. The first brown leaves were already on the ground. Autumn always brings melancholy and depression, but there is nothing like it. The beauty of the nature, the smell of the air. I get easily distracted, truth be told, but this time my curiosity surpassed my wandering mind.

I opened the envelope carefully. There was a piece of folded paper inside and a black notebook with its edges torn, the pages bent and wrinkled, and the spine sacked.

I unfolded the letter and read,

Dear Ellen,

We haven't spoken since forever. I take a little blame in that. I hope you're doing fine. How is your writing inspiration? You must be wondering why I am sending you a letter and what this notebook is. I found it on a bridge while chasing down its owner. You will understand better when you read it. I'm planning to visit you by the end of the month. Please read carefully and let me know your thoughts. I couldn't think of another person to send this to. These are the kinds of things I'm dealing with almost every day at work, so you can imagine why I'm not able to keep in touch with almost anyone I know.

See you soon, my little friend.

Lots of love,
Luck

I read the black notebook three times. Only one word came to mind. Salvation. There comes a time when a person's life can be compared to a rotten apple. Red and shiny on the outside, bruised and filthy on the inside. The longer it lives, the faster it decays. In such a condition, you have no choice but to throw the apple away. In such a condition, you have no choice but to end the life.

No one can judge a disturbed mind and its actions. The brain in fear can produce a plethora of paranoid ideas that lead to dangerous paths. It is often said that there is a thin red line between logic and paranoia and this line is called life. When life challenges you repeatedly, all you need is a little push to go astray. Are we to blame for our choices or is everything in our life affected by others?

I don't know the past of the black notebook's owner, but I know his present.

1

PARIS, FRANCE

My journey to France would be best described as bittersweet.

It was the end of June. It was that time of the year when summer begins to control both body and mind. My senses were free from any sadness, darkness, self-pity, and boredom. And although this celebration of freedom and relaxation would be ideal in a place with an endless ocean, I decided my first destination of this summer to be in a busy city, like Paris.

Being alone on a deserted island would certainly relax me and give me time to process everything that had happened to me so far this year. And this was exactly what I did not want. What I really wanted was a place full of people, a busy city to keep my mind off the depression I've been dealing with.

The first half of this year was not the best anyone could ask for.

Not the best – What a polite way to describe a divorce, a bankruptcy, and an unsuccessful suicide! But I had the feeling that this year was about to change. This is what summer does to you. It takes you to this euphoric state where you think that anything can be possible.

I am not sure when I last took a trip on my own. I used to plan all my trips with my ex-wife. To be honest, she would plan, and I was just along for the ride. But I would never complain, in fact whining and complaining was her specialty.

Traveling alone was something strange and new. And although Paris is considered to be the most romantic city in the world, I was sure I would enjoy it better on my own. It seemed that the company of others had a negative impact on me and vice versa.

They say Paris is the city of light. Millions of little sparkles cause the dense mass of old, dirty buildings look like glitter in a canvas. Little cafés pop out in every corner. Parks, lakes, and of course tremendous historical artifacts. The Eiffel Tower, Musée de Louvre (pronouncing it with the French accent that my beloved friend Charline tried so hard to teach me) and of course Notre Dame Cathedral. The place where all began.

On the second day of July, I arrived in Paris, having left Greece behind – my most beloved, and at the same time, most hated place. As soon as I set foot on French soil, I felt totally different. So familiar and safe, so warm and relaxed. I had a minor disadvantage and that was my French. I vaguely remembered one or two words from school. As much as I wanted to feel and look like a Parisian citizen, everything about me would scream tourist.

Center of Paris. I settled in a small motel, so dark and scary on the outside, but so warm and friendly on the inside. That motel was exactly what I needed. The owner, a fat lady, quite beautiful in the face, but definitely single, I thought, offered her assistance. She gave me a travel guide for the city, the phone number of a taxi driver in case I got lost and of course an advertising brochure that had every little detail about her small motel.

"Is this your first time in France?" her English accent was perfect. So perfect that I almost envied it and tried to answer as perfectly as I could.

"It is. And I am totally thrilled."

"But sir, you have not seen anything yet. When it gets dark, Paris becomes a different city. It is no coincidence that our city was named La Ville-Lumière."

I was impressed. Every new piece of information, every little discovery can make me feel alive. Awakens my soul. The truth is that I get bored very easily. Everything... the routine tires me... bothers me. When your life has been built on dry land, you always seek a new life in the furious waves of the ocean. So, I would seek for the drama. I would cause the drama in my life. Otherwise, I cannot live.

"Are you staying many days?"

"I don't know yet. It depends on Paris itself." I smiled at the nice owner whose name was Annie and we walked together to my room. A small but cozy place to spend my Parisian days. Everything was perfect. I took a quick shower, got dressed, and left straight away to explore the city. I'm not used to carry a lot of things on me, so my wallet, my camera, and the travel guide that Annie gave me, would be enough for my excursion.

I walked for hours and yet I didn't feel exhausted. Everything was perfect. Maybe I had extra optimism and an inexplicable enthusiasm for seeing everything so dreamy. In other circumstances, I might had been locked in a motel room or playing cards with Annie at the front desk. But no! A little optimism and positive energy in my thirties could not hurt me even if it was going to last for a while.

It was late afternoon. The sky had an orange shade that hypnotized me. The golden hour, they say! I was standing under the Notre Dame Cathedral in Paris, enchanted by the majesty. It was the reflection of the sunset on the imposing building that I knew heaven had touched the Earth. As I was gazing at every inch of the Cathedral, I imagined Quasimodo hiding up there in the bell tower. To wander around it made me think of a younger version of me that, like the character of V. Hugo's book, feeling a prisoner in his own life but with no need of escape…

"Pardon, s'il vous plait," a thin female voice spoke in French interrupting the sweet recollection of my childhood.

"Yes?" I answered in English, showing once again that I am a tourist.

"Can you take a picture of us, please?" asked the young man next to her in English.

"Of course," I answered. The happy couple took different poses, showing to the camera how much in love they were. I tried my best to capture all the prodigious love on this magical moment. Not to brag about it, but the photo was wonderful. I took a step toward them, smiling. It was at that moment that incidents like the following made me wish the ground could open, drag me inside, and make me disappear from this world. I stumbled, fell, and broke the couple's camera. Fortunately, mine was in its case and didn't get a scratch. Every cloud has a silver lining, so I had to think of mine.

The young man ran toward me, furious, shouting some incomprehensible words in French that were definitely not compliments. The girl was picking up the parts of the broken camera without saying a word. I think I blacked out for a moment – no talking, no watching, no thinking, no nothing. It was the sudden pain in my right hand that brought me back to reality. The angry young man had grabbed me by the arm and shook me hard, cursing me in French. I tried in vain to explain since his voice would have covered the sound of the bells that Quasimodo had rung from the temple next to us. People laughed at us and all I wanted was to be back in the motel and play cards with Annie. It would not be such a bad idea after all.

And while I was wondering what else could I have possibly done to avoid this unfortunate moment, as well as the assaults of my attacker, a tall, blond-hair man approached. He came between us and pulled the angry man away from me. While they were arguing, always in French, I was palpating my arm, sure that it had been bruised. I saw that a fight might break out, so I brought the whole dramatic scene to an end. I took 200€ out of my wallet and gave it to the young man. I apologized for my carelessness that cost them their camera. I knew the price of the camera, since I had once the same model, and the money was more than enough. The young man grabbed the money and left.

"Are you ok?" the blond man asked me in English.

"Yes. Thank you very much for everything," I said, holding my shoulder.

"We saw the whole scene, and when we

realized that the young man was out of control, we ran to help you. Not your best experience from our city, eh?" The young girl who was talking to me was obviously the blonde man's partner who had rescued me. She had a French accent and I could hardly understand some words.

"I arrived today. Usually, I'm not so careless. It was my bad luck, I guess. Thank you very much again."

"First day? Well, that's not the best way to start your vacation."

"I decided to make a journey – well five, to be precise – to different cities in Europe this summer and I decided my first destination to be France."

The excited couple kept asking me more and more things about my journey and my life. Excited myself, and having forgotten the unfortunate event, I asked for more information about Paris. We ended up in a pub and before we knew it, we all watched the sunrise together.

I learned almost everything about the adorable couple, Charline and Thomas.

Charline was a cute, pencil-thin blonde, born in Lyon, a small town in France. Thomas was from Madrid, where they now lived permanently. They were both teachers. They had come to Paris for a few days on holiday and then they would spend the rest of their vacation with Charline's parents in Lyon.

We exchanged telephone numbers and they even offered to take me on a tour of Paris for the rest of my stay. Of course, I accepted since I rarely like people on the first sight.

I wouldn't call myself a superstitious person but meeting new people because of an unfortunate incident does not sound a particularly promising beginning to a new acquaintance or even friendship. And yet life surprises you.

I went back to my motel, exhausted. I saw Annie at reception, and I waved with a friendly smile. She waved back and continued talking on the phone. I lay on my comfortable bed and opened the tourist guide. There were so many little spots I hadn't yet seen. France was for sure the number one destination in Europe. I don't know if it was the place itself or my two sweet friends, but it was the first time, – after a very long time, that I enjoyed the company of other people. I kept a few notes about the sights that I was more interested in, and I sent a message to Thomas in case they wanted to accompany me to any of those the next day.

The following days passed quickly. I explored every little corner of Paris, and I learned many new French words that I did not miss the opportunity to repeat here and there. Narrow streets crowded with people rushing to go to work, restaurants, cafés… oh, the little cafés… popping up on every corner, designed as if they were part of a romantic 19th century movie. There were architecturally amazing buildings in the center of the city that the French would preserve with such respect and grace through the ages – something that my country could not or did not want to do. This is what I liked about Paris, the beauty of life.

I always had the lovable couple by my side. A strong friendship had been born and would surely last. It still holds… at least in my heart. It is a wonder how fate brings some people to your life. And you can't help but feel blessed and enjoy the little things because you never know what might happen.

I remember one night – like every other night – we were dining in a spectacular restaurant with a panoramic view of the whole city, and in the middle of it all the magnificent Tower would amaze us with its hundreds of little lights. Charline confessed to me how much she would like to have a baby. She had discussed it with Thomas and, at first, he was negative about it due to their financial problems. She asked me to bring up the topic about babies on a quiet, wine-filled afternoon, just so she could see his reaction. However, due to a lot of alcohol and a lot of my nonstop monologues about almost any insignificant topic one could imagine, the talk about babies never happened. But I promised Charlene that I would do it very soon when the opportunity arose.

I should have done it then. I had promised her that. Of course, the difference whether I had done it then or later would be absolutely none.

The day that the beautiful couple had to leave for Lyon had arrived. Their last words to me were,

"We hope to see you soon. If you decide to come to Lyon the next days, we can leave all together for Madrid as we said."

I was so happy. For a few moments I felt like I was surrounded by people that create this unexpected feeling of joy and calmness you need in life. I was thinking that when I visited them, it would be the perfect opportunity for me to bring up the baby talk. I was thinking how lovely it would be, to meet Charline's family. To get to know more about this perfect couple. But as I said before, life surprises you.

Their train would leave at 17.15 from Paris to Lyon. I wanted so badly to accompany them to the station, but Annie requested my help with plumbing a leak… disaster, more like. I consider myself an expert in all little mechanical problems. Of course, as it turned out after three hours of messing up the pipes, we had to call a plumber. He finished everything in almost twenty minutes, and we walked back to the lobby. We encountered a group of people screaming and shouting and dialing numbers on their phones again and again, and I was about to find out what all this endless distress was about.

There are times when pain becomes your worst enemy. It crushes you from the inside out. It leaves you helpless. You want to scream, but your voice is drowned at the depths of your soul. You want to cry, but the tears are frozen. You wonder why, but even the smallest thought turns into chaos. And all that's left is a man staring into space with sweat running from his body.

"Are you ok, sir?" The plumber's voice brought me back to reality. My ears were ringing, and I could hardly hear the conversation around me. I looked for a chair to sit. Even looking and trying to identify an object in the room seemed like a difficult activity to me. When I finally came to my senses, I listened carefully to what, at that moment, hoped, was a lie.

"THE 17.14 TRAIN FROM PARIS
TO LYON, WAS DERAILED
AND CRASHED 45 MIINUTES
AFTER ITS DEPARTURE. THE
TOLL STANDS AT 6 DEATHS
AND DOZENS OF INJURIES.
THE SURVIVORS ARE
SPEAKING ABOUT A
TERRIFYING, VIOLENT
EXPERIENCE, ESPECIALLY
FOR THOSE WHO WERE IN
WAGON 3, FOUND 10KM AWAY
FROM THE REST OF THE
TRAIN..."

I didn't know what to do. I started calling my beloved friends. I had the desperate need to hear their voices. To make sure that they are okay. After the sixth time with no response, I asked for Annie's phone just to make sure that nothing was wrong with mine. I even thought of buying a brand-new phone, as if the new one would give me the answer I was looking for. A man, in need of hope, can think of the craziest things to do in order to escape and buy some time, instead of dealing with reality. Needless to say, both phones were working perfectly and from neither of them, have I gotten any reply!

The whole day passed like this. No news, no information about the accident, no nothing. I could feel that little burn in my breast, that little pinch in my stomach. I could not find a single drop of hope inside me that everything will be okay. That my friends were all right. That they had just experienced a terrible accident, and they were trying to calm down. Maybe they were trying to find a way to call me and reassure me that everything was ok. That in a few days we would be all together, as discussed, and have the baby talk that I had promised to Charline. This was how much self-centered I was – two people that have just experienced something so terrible would think of me as their first person to contact with.

Late at night and while sleep was miles away, the names of the passengers who lost their lives on the train derailment were announced. Within a few hours the names were everywhere, on the internet, in the newspapers, on the radio. Among the names were two familiar ones:

Charline Zid and Toma Molinde.

"Have courage for the great sorrows in life, and patience for the small ones. And when you have laboriously accomplished your daily tasks, go to sleep in peace, God is awake." - Victor Hugo

2

MADRID, SPAIN

I would describe my trip to Spain as incredibly tragic.

I had been in Madrid for a week and I had not left the hotel. I had chosen Spain as my next destination. Where else could I go?

To find optimism, look for the happy things in life. What optimism? There is nothing in this life, absolutely nothing that you can be happy about. And even if there is, it would last a moment. There is only injustice and a big *why*?

The very next day after the tragic event in France, I left. I didn't even have the chance to say goodbye to Annie properly. I left like a thief in the night. My whole body hurts. I've been lying in the same bed for seven days. Everything appears black and hazy. 35 degrees outside and I was shivering all over. I was scared. It was one of the few emotions that I could easily recognize and accept. Accept it and let it swallow me.

I knew this couple for ten days and yet it was as if I had known them for a lifetime. Even when I got divorced after fifteen years of marriage, I was not this upset. I haven't seen my ex-wife, nor have I spoken to her, since the last time I saw her in our lawyer's office. I have no idea where she was, what she did, if she was married again. I didn't even know if she was alive. Fifteen years of shared life with a person, and I didn't know if they were alive. What kind of person did that make me? Was this the right time to feel remorse? I had become so attached to this young couple because it was the only good thing that had happened to me for an awfully long time and their own journey ended so suddenly, so unfairly, and brutally. They say that a journey never really ends even if we've reached our destination, because the memory continues living on inside of us.

My thoughts were interrupted by the sound of the wooden door. I got up and walked, almost crawled into the huge room I was staying in alone. I opened the door. An old lady with a hunch, wearing a black uniform was standing in front of me. She looked like an ugly witch.

"What do you want?" I asked aggressively.

"I am here to clean." she answered me in the same style.

Without even letting me answer, she pulled out a huge, black garbage bag and entered the room. She opened the balcony door and started wiping. I lay on the bed again and continued to look at the ceiling.

"You will die soon."

"Excuse me?" I thought I misunderstood, but the old woman repeated the same phrase to me.

"And how do you know that?" I asked her angrily as she once again interrupted my thoughts.

"You are alone. Loneliness kills you. First it drives you crazy and then it kills you."

"And I was worried that my smoking would kill me." I smiled because I managed to make a lame joke, my first in over a week. I sat up to make my pillow more comfortable. She did not laugh at my joke. She remained serious and was not distracted from her job. She piqued my interest. As it turned out, it was exactly what I needed. In order to forget about my friends' deaths, I had to talk about my own death.

"I've been alone for 35 years and I am full of life. I do not see myself dying any day soon," I said, wanting to continue the conversation, but she did not answer. She put the old dirty broom aside and started mopping. The room had already begun to smell like lavender. I actually started noticing the little things, like the beautiful red painting hanged on the wall, the ridiculously big lamp next to a leather green armchair. There was still life around me, I had just chosen not to see it. The old woman continued to ignore me. But the more she ignored me, the more I wanted to speak with her. I could not stop looking at her. I observed her face, her body, her movements, and I guessed she was younger than she looked, but hard life sometimes leaves a big scar on you whether is visible or not. Her whole body leaned forward and the hunch on her back was evidence of how difficult this kind of job was for her. However, she looked so strong and confident, like she could run a marathon and win.

"I'm not afraid of loneliness," I finally answered, but still no response, "but death yes."

The old woman raised her head and looked at me. It was this phrase, these three words that awakened her.

"Christ defeated death with his own death, so that we can all live peacefully without fear," she answered me.

Great! Another crazy religious old woman, I thought.

"Get up!" she screamed.

"What?"

"Get up!"

"What do you want?"

"To change the sheets," she answered. I got up and went to the bathroom, while smiling stupidly. My beard had grown a lot and I looked sloppy and tired, and yet in the last week I had slept more than I had slept the whole year. I took a shower and shaved. My reflection in the mirror was that of a stranger. Was this person me? I was the same on the outside, but something felt unfamiliar. Something had changed me. I must have been looking myself in the mirror for more than hour - looking but not actually seeing. I had forgotten the old woman and when I came out, she was gone.

I got dressed and, for the first time in a week, I felt the need to explore the new city I was in. I started with one goal; to make five journeys. That was my resolution for this year, to explore five different places and there I was on my second trip, and I had already given up.

I went to the hotel lobby and saw the old cleaning lady again. She was surrounded by a group of young people that were teasing her. I laughed and continued walking towards the exit looking at them, when my gaze stumbled upon hers. The way she looked at me was so... so... I could not explain it. I felt numb. I felt my entire body tremble. I felt the need to help her. I ran straight to them and advised them to leave the old woman alone before they got themselves in real trouble. The young people, unexpectedly friendly with me, obeyed and left laughing. The old woman without even looking at me, without even saying thank you, took the black bag full of garbage that she was dragging around the hotel and disappeared. I stayed still and thought about her. Something had drawn me to her. From the first moment I saw her entering my room, I knew that something strange was happening or would happen.

That day I explored the city of Madrid. Nothing looked the same as my first day in Paris. The streets, although crowded, felt empty and quiet. Walking down Gran Via street, the most central avenue in the city, felt like walking in the narrowest and darkest alley. To pedestrians, I was nothing more than a regular man, with a predictable behavior and a common look, but as an observer of my own being I could tell that this man could not fit in. He could not be part of anything. It was pointless to walk endless hours in a city that could bring about unpleasant memories and unruly feelings. I returned to the hotel and decided to stay there for as long as I needed it.

I needed just a few more days as it turned out, and everything was starting to feel normal again, if normal is the word to use. I will never forget that day. What I experienced was indescribable, almost unbelievable. But not as unbelievable as what happened 24 hours later.

I heard voices outside my room. I looked at my watch and it was eight o'clock in the morning. People are crazy. I was still half asleep and yet some people had managed to get up, get dressed, apparently eat breakfast – there was no other explanation for someone to have so much energy at eight o'clock in the morning – come out of their room and start fighting.

I got up and opened the door. The hotel manager and a chubby lady were in the hall shouting. Standing in the middle silently was the old cleaning lady that kept visiting my room every single day. The whole corridor was full of hotel guests. They were peeking out of rooms, listening indiscreetly. "Curiosity has its own reason for existence," Albert Einstein once said – and so does gossip, I dare add. From what I could hear, the chubby lady was accusing the old cleaning woman of stealing something from her room. The manager tried to convince her that such a thing would be impossible. The old cleaning lady did not make a fuss. She was staring at the floor with her arms crossed. I felt sorry for her. The manager was desperately explaining to his upset guest that it was impossible for Mary – that was her name – to have done such a thing. According to him, Mary had worked for that hotel for over 20 years and they trusted her. I heard him say,

"It is more likely for someone to blame

me for stealing and be right than blaming Mary."

"Well, this is what they do. People like her. They gain your trust, so you have no doubt of them and then they take action. If you do not find the people responsible, which for sure is her, I will call the police. I will sue you. This will not end well." The voice of the chubby woman – probably rich considering the dozens of golden jewelries on her– was so irritating that with every word coming out of her mouth, I was one step closer of bursting out from anger. However, it was three, specific words that made me completely furious – people like her.

I could always understand why children are mean to each other – why they say words that offend each other, they say things that hurt each other, they do things that cause real pain, but what I could never understand was why educated adults with lots of experiences in life – good or bad – would intentionally do something like that to one another. What is this evil inside one's mind that wishes this harm on another's heart?

I was terribly upset, and I felt the need to defend Mary once again. I didn't know what made me do the following, which I would regret for the rest of my life. I left the room and approached the noisy people who had awakened me and ruined my morning.

"Sorry to interrupt, but can you explain to me why you have distressed the whole hotel?"

"Forgive me, sir, but if you have fallen victim of theft, you would act the same way. I spent so much money to stay in such a hotel exactly because I thought it would be safe and secure for a person like me and this is how they treat me."

A person like me. Who did she think she was? It was one of those moments when you know that you hate a person before you even learn their name.

"This woman here," she continued, pointing empathetically at Mary, "stole a dress from me." I wore it last night and I remember I left it on the chair next to the desk. After this woman cleaned my room my dress was gone."

"My lady, what can an old woman with a hunch do with your dress?" I asked. It was so ridiculous what I was hearing. The manager laughed discreetly. Obviously, we all understood the exaggeration in the lady's reaction.

"She may have a daughter. I don't know and I don't care. I want it back."

"Mary, did you take the dress?" I asked, calling her by her name for the first time. Mary raised her head and looked at me. Through the whole conversation, she didn't look away from the floor. It was as if she was looking for something, like something small of size but great of value that had fallen from her hands, and was carefully looking down at the same spot to find it. She answered a heartbroken "No."

"Don't believe her. She is a thief. I'm telling you, she's a thief," repeated. She was out of control and her frustration could no longer stay verbal. She approached the poor woman, pushed her hard and threw her down onto her back. Everyone was stunned by this spectacle. Without wasting time and without thinking, I gave a strong push to the chubby lady, who stumbled and almost fallen. The hotel manager and two other hotel guests helped Mary get up. Twenty minutes later, I was detained at the central police station.

The hotel I was staying in was one of the largest in Madrid and a lot of important people were guests, which meant no scandals, no publicity. God knew who this monster who called herself human being was, but to avoid any scandal, I was taken to the police station. I would be detained for two days, then I would be free to leave. It was the first time I was in jail. The policemen were very friendly and helpful. In fact, they laughed and mocked the absurd behavior of that woman, whom I never learned the name of, but my guess would be something between Lucifer and Frankenstein.

I've read in books that spending a night in a cell is a traumatic experience. The isolation and the darkness surround you and the outside world feels like a utopia. For me that was not the case. The freedom of every individual is objective. There are people who committed suicide in prison because they could not deal with the isolation. There are people who took advantage of the peace and created works of art. As an ancient Greek historian once said, "The desire for freedom is inherent in all people."

For me, however, that was not the case. In order to be able to feel something, I must, first, be able to define it. And what the word freedom meant to me after everything I went through, I cannot define. All I know is that the sticky, dark cell felt closer to my ideal freedom than the magical, outside world where I had to deal with everyone and everything. Lying on the bed of the hotel looking at the ceiling was an everyday ritual which could not help me deal with what I'd been through. Sitting in the corner of the dark cell and staring into nothing could make me feel more alive and liberated than I'd ever been in years. At that point, I thought that my actions that led me to this cold, dark hole were in my benefit, but I'm used to being wrong.

The day came when I was released and left my ideal freedom behind. Life was still happening, people kept going at the same stressful and fast pace while I had managed to successfully escape to what people call the good life. Life does not care if something happens to you. It goes on – like when my two good friends lost their lives. Nothing changed around me. Nobody changed because of this. Nobody stopped working, nobody stayed locked in their room crying, or thinking for endless hours. Nobody. Days felt like years since the fatal accident. How can I feel so far away from it and yet the scars are more intense than ever?

Again, my thoughts did not allow me to enjoy the colorful journey back to the hotel. I did not look, not once, outside the cab's window. Before I knew it, I had arrived at the hotel, ready to pack my things and be off to the next adventure. There was one thing I needed to do before I went, however. I had this great confidence and feeling, no more misery or depression, but something felt wrong. It was like people could not appreciate this euphoric state of mine and I was bothered by that. They could not feel empathy when I was depressed or joyous.

"Good morning! I would like to pay for the days I stayed here. My name is…"

"How are you, sir?" the clerk asked me.

"I've been better," I replied. "Do you know where Mary lives?"

"Mary? Mary who?"

"Oh, I'm sorry. I should have been more specific. There is an old woman who cleaned my room named Mary."

The clerk rolled his eyes. He took a sad look and said, "Mary… was… was on the train." The sound of the word train took away every merry bit I had inside of me and replaced it with a pain in my chest.

"Which train?"

"She was coming to visit you yesterday, but how could you know? She was on the train."

"Where was she going? The police station? She never came. And on which train?"

"On *the* train, but you do not know about yesterday's events?"

"I do not understand you, my dear man. Please explain." I felt irritated and, at the same time, worried. I wanted to punch this man. He kept repeating the word train without any explanation. Something had happened. The more he repeated the word, the more I shivered.

"Yesterday, Mary asked for two days off for the first time in the twenty years that she's been working here. It seemed strange, since she did not appear sick at all. Besides, even when she was had been given permission for a vacation, she preferred to stay here. But of course, after the incident with the stupid guest who wouldn't want a few days off. She was very lonely and weird, if you will, in my opinion."

I became dissatisfied, and the reaction on my face showed him that I did not care about his gossip and opinion, but facts. The man understood my irritation.

"So, I asked her what had happened, and she wanted two days off. She told me she wanted to go to Ferrol, where you were, and see you. To thank you, I guess. So, she took the afternoon train and…"

At that moment, I felt a buzz in my ears and a shiver through my body. The hairs of my body stood up. It was as if it was in the middle of winter and somebody had opened a window and all the cold air had flooded into the hotel. I didn't know what I was going to hear. Or did I?

"The train, on which Mary was on, derailed. Many were injured, and ten people died. The police informed us that Mary was… was one of them."

I felt my heart stop.

"I'm very sorry," he told me. I could not speak.

I was speechless for two minutes. The clerk looked at me without speaking. Unconsciously, I took a random amount of money out of my wallet, gave it to the clerk and said,

"Are we okay?" He looked at me strangely.

"For the room… are we okay?" I repeated.

Two hours later, I was at the airport, looking at the flight schedules one by one. I could not move from the chair on which I had collapsed. I felt so weak, almost paralyzed. So much noise inside a huge airport and I was able to hear my heart beating close to my chest. Millions of thoughts in my mind. My head was going to explode.

She had come to see me.

She had wanted to see me.

She died because of me.

If I hadn't been in jail, if I had not hit that woman, if I was not involved, if I had not left my room that morning, if I was not in Spain…

And then I remembered the reason I had come to Spain. Charline and Thomas. They were killed in a train derailment. The exact same way.

"It's my fault! It's my fault," I whispered to myself.

I wiped my forehead. Sweat was dripping from everywhere. Without thinking, I ran to the toilet to splash some water on my face, leaving my things unattended. The same reflection in the mirror, the same stranger appeared, like the morning when I first met Mary in my hotel room. I did not feel anything. People in the restroom looked at me strangely as if I were a junkie. I did not have the time to feel bad about that, so I quickly returned to my seat. My suitcases were at the same place, only now, a family of tourists was sitting next to me. They spoke in English. Of course, the topic of their discussion was the tragic incident with the train.

"I heard it on the news today. It was the conductor's fault," the father said.

"I heard there was a mechanical problem," the mother answered.

The couple talked for a long time, arguing about what really happened at the train accident and all I was thinking was,

Which conductor? What problem? It's my fault. Do you hear me? It's my fault.

The little girl of the family was stood right in front of me and looked into my eyes. She was holding a doll that was missing one eye. She was holding her as if it were her baby and was trying to protect it. She was not doing a particularly good job, since the doll had already lost one of her eyes and her white dress was a colorful mess. Sometimes no matter how much you love someone, you can never completely protect them. The little girl stared at me for more than two minutes, which could mean one particular thing. She sensed something. I took my suitcases and walked away. It wasn't in my imagination, people kept looking at me. They could see the guilt in my eyes. I wasn't crazy! Right?

"A guilty conscience needs to confess." - Albert Camus

3

ZURICH, SWITZERLAND

I would describe my trip to Switzerland as quite short.

I was a mess when I got there. I wanted to leave Spain as soon as possible and Switzerland was the first and cheapest flight on the board. I couldn't hesitate any longer. I couldn't stay in a place where guilt and psychotic thoughts surrounded me. I had the illusion that by the time I arrived in Switzerland, I would forget everything. Charline, Thomas, Mary. Three people that, a month ago, I did not even know I would meet, in two places that I did not even know I would be. They stayed so briefly in my life and yet they marked it forever. And they would not be the only ones.

I left my things at the first hotel I found near the airport and went to a restaurant to have a bite. Almost 24 hours had passed without having eaten. I had a constant pinching in my stomach. It felt like butterflies, however, it wasn't love that gave me this feeling. Maybe it was a predictable feeling of sadness or an unexpected fear of paranoia.

The electronic sign of the store opposite the restaurant where I was sitting read: 9pm / 26-7-2013. The days flowed, the hours, the minutes. So many things have happened and yet time did not stop to grieve, to be shocked, to be disappointed, to get angry, to shout; it just kept going. I was thinking of what a co-worker had told me after my divorce, "Life goes on, buddy. What are you going to do? Life goes on." It is somewhat ironic to think that after the bankruptcy of the company in which we worked, he attempted suicide. An unsuccessful one. He failed, just like my sister had. And here was another tragic irony. Life was given to those ungrateful ones. It did not give up on them. However, for my three friends - yes Mary is my friend - life had other plans.

"No one lives the life he chooses to live."

But is, in fact, everything predetermined? Or is it just random? Coincidences of life? Do our choices determine the life we will live? Or no matter what we choose the result will be the same?

The chicken fillet I ate was awful. I don't remember the name of the restaurant. I don't even know if the chef himself was to blame for what I ate or just myself. Whatever I put in my mouth had no taste.

Does life really go on? Was there a lesson I needed to learn? Was there a hidden message from all these that would teach me how to appreciate people and life? Should I take advantage of what was at least given to me? So many thoughts back then. I had not yet learned my lesson.

The next day around noon, I found an internet café for an online search to find out more about the two accidents. It triggered my curiosity. Two similar accidents in two different places that I happened to be and with my friends on board. I could not let it go and move on. This constant overthinking and searching and analyzing was destroying me, yet I could not help but do so. I did not even know exactly what I was looking for or what more I wanted to know. It was as if I was trying to find a time machine that could bring my friends back. A time machine that would make me go back and change everything I'd done.

"Isn't what happened terrible?" said a female British voice. I did not answer. I assumed she was not talking to me. She repeated the same thing in the exact same tone, as if it were the first time she did. A brunette, petite, and beautiful lady was staring at me with shining eyes and awaiting my answer.

"Excuse me?" I managed to say.

"I was in Madrid when the train derailed. It was terrible."

"Yes," I answered indifferently, avoiding

eye contact. But what did she want? The last thing I wanted was to catch up with a stranger about the latest news of the insanity I was living in. Couldn't she understand that it was annoying?

"Have you heard anything new?"

"That's what I'm searching for."

"It was terrible. I can only imagine how you must be feeling when you had someone of your own on the train." I rolled my eyes and looked at her.

"No. I had nobody," I answered. Who was this girl? Did she know me? Did she see me in Madrid? Was she watching me? Did she know about Mary?

"Oh, really? Me neither. I was in Madrid for a job just for a few days. I was so close to the accident that day. And to think that I use the train all the time." The pretty girl realized that I was no longer interested in continuing conversation.

"I'm probably bothering you though. I'm sorry. Goodbye"

As soon as I felt her body rise and move away from me, I shouted,

"No, no. Please! Talk to me."

I could not believe what I was saying. I wanted to be alone. Every interaction, every communication, every word could compromise my entire life. Nonetheless, I wanted this girl to talk to me. Her voice calmed me down. Maybe I wanted to confess, maybe I wanted to hear someone telling me that it wasn't my fault, that everything was going to be okay. But just when I thought that my atonement was close, she turned and said,

"My name is Mary."

That was it. No, this was not accidental. This encounter was not accidental. Life was not random. This was a sign. Her name was a sign. I didn't know why yet somehow, I had to take advantage of it.

Now, of course, I know I should have gotten up and left the same day —not just from the café but from the country itself. I should have avoided this meeting with this girl, and I should have avoided any contact this summer. I should have followed my original plan, and finished these journeys all by myself. Calm, relaxed and most importantly alone.

As the hours passed, I became more and more attached to this girl, and I had the longing to tell her everything. I wanted an answer. I needed her to help me. It was this single person who could give me a bit of faith, a drop of hope. As soon as I heard the words that I so wanted to hear from someone, then I would calm down. The words that would relief my consciousness and make able again to continue my travels, as I had planned from the beginning. *Everything is going to be all right. It wasn't your fault.* I knew this girl was the answer to my problems.

"I cannot believe it. You must be devastated. That's unbearable," replied Mary, after hearing my story. After our first meeting in the café, we kept in touch and I invited for dinner the next evening. She had not touched her food or her glass of wine while listening to my story. Once again it was not the restaurant to blame. It was a cozy, warm restaurant, with no more than a few tables and a lightning unnecessarily low, almost romantic. I could not wait any longer, I had to get it all off my chest and Mary would be my pillow of comfort.

I told her everything that had happened to me. I could hear myself speaking and I felt like I was describing a movie I had just seen. Even I could not believe that I was 'involved' in something like this. I felt like I was no longer… normal. It was as if my spirit has left my body and there I was, without controlling any of my senses, just looking at a soulless body. I was just… existing. Like a puppet who needed her creator to act and breath. The problem was that I was still looking for who my creator was.

"I imagine when you heard my name…" said Mary.

Suddenly, I couldn't hear anything. My brain restarted, like a computer, to save and process all the actions that have been made. Thirty-five years of my insignificant life, I never believed in luck or coincidences. Why do it now? There must have been a reason for everything that happened, a logical explanation. And finally, all these pieces of a yet unfinished puzzle of my life made sense to somebody else. And it was totally… normal. No, I wasn't crazy. Because that would mean she was crazy as well.

"Are you ok?" Mary asked me.

"Yes, sorry. I tend to do that sometimes," I answered sharply.

"Do what?"

"Get lost in my thoughts and disappear mentally from the real world."

"You are terribly quite since we left the restaurant."

"Where are you from?" I stopped walking. We were on our way to the hotel. She was staying in a small motel a few meters away from mine.

"But I told you, I'm from Newcastle."

"And what are you doing here?"

"Didn't you hear me talking to you?"

"Yes. I'm sorry, I'm not feeling very well," I replied, trying to remember the whole story about her life. Most of the night we spent was already erased in my mind. As if it never happened. My spirit was again absent.

"How did you know I'm not from here?" I continued.

"Excuse me?"

"You knew I was a tourist."

"What do you mean I knew that?"

"At the café you approached me and spoke to me in English."

"Oh… um, as I was leaving the café, I couldn't help but notice you. I looked at your computer screen and saw that you were reading the article about the train in English. I was so upset by the incident and curious to see another person interested in it."

Somehow, I wasn't entirely convinced, but I couldn't care less. I couldn't even remember why she cared so much about this incident with the train. Did she have a relative of her own? Did she lose someone on that train too? Everything was blurry. All that mattered to me was that I had found someone who could understand me.

"Okay This is your hotel. I guess this is a goodnight." I said and turned to leave.

"One second, please. I have an idea."

I looked at her curiously.

"How about we go for brunch tomorrow?"

"What?"

"It was so strange that we met under these circumstances but I'm glad. I know you will refuse, but I promise not to ask you any strange questions about... the subject. I also have a small interview late afternoon in a small town just outside Bern. We can go together. I know it's a bit too much, we've just met, but I think it will be good for both of us. You will have someone to talk to or not, whatever, and I could use some company right before my interview. So, what do you think?"

"I don't know... I..."

Her eyes sparkled as though she were trying to hypnotize me, to convince me to follow her. I knew my answer the minute she asked. I was not ready to be separated from this woman. Not just yet.

"So? I'm picking you up at twelve. Deal?" she smiled with a great confidence.

"Yes, okay."

"Mary?"

She turned and looked at me afraid that I would cancel.

"What time is your interview? Is it ok to meet in the afternoon?"

"Yes. My interview is at five o'clock. I guess we can meet around two, at the train station. I will also get the tickets. Do not be late. Have a good night." She left smiling.

It was the last time I saw her. Why would I suggest meeting in the afternoon? I had nothing to do in the morning. I could easily go on this trip in the morning. Yet, something inside me ordered me to change the time and do it in the afternoon. Why? She was innocent. In the end, she was just another innocent person.

I could not sleep at all that night. My overthinking had now reached its peak. God knew if I could find just a moment of peace in my mind and enjoy a simple moment. God? Now that I think of it, no, God doesn't know anything. I lay in bed awake and agitated. The last time I looked at my watch, it was nine o'clock in the morning. Of course, when I finally fell asleep, nothing could wake me up. I was so exhausted these past few days that when my body managed to give in, it was hard to come back. I had fallen into a deep sleep, fortunately without dreams or nightmares, even though my subconscious was full of monstrous thoughts that turned into grotesque images in my mind.

I opened my eyes and checked the time. Nine o'clock in the evening. I jumped up and grabbed my cell phone. Three messages and twelve calls. Oh my God. Mary. The interview. What will she think of me? I did not even look at the messages on my agitation. I tried to call her in vain. No ringing, no nothing.

I got up, splashed some water on my face and tried to call her again. No success. Was she so upset that she hung up her cell phone? She must have been back at her hotel by now. Without second thoughts, I ran to the reception to find out if anyone had left a message for me. The cheerful receptionist smiled at me. I turned my head just for a second and glanced at the big screen on the right. It was the evening news and a big headline in red letters:

TRAIN FROM ZURICH TO BERN DERAILED AT 17.25.

30 INJURIES, 5 DEATHS.

I felt the need to sit down. It was at this moment that I realized for the first time in my life that I had to think, only this time it would be with my conscience. Once I sat on the dark-red-colored couch in the hotel's lounge, I looked around me. I was all alone. The monstrous thoughts surrounded me again and I felt like I was drowning. I tried to wave them away, like an annoying mosquito flying around me. I still possessed the ability to do that, back then.

There was no time for panicking. I retraced the steps one by one. I agreed to accompany Mary for her interview, I had overslept due to my insomnia the night before, well, of course who could blame me? When a person experiences what I had in the past few days, insomnia would seem like a positive side effect. But again, I am overthinking while writing with no control. Where was I? I overslept… and by the time I woke up, Mary was probably back home. It could have happened to anyone. With an enormous bouquet of pink roses, I would sincerely apologize to her and everything would be okay. It was not like she had missed her interview because of me. She would have gone either way. So, she didn't miss anything.

"What do you mean she's missing since this morning?" The receptionist at the hotel where Mary was staying, informed me that she had left early this morning and had not yet returned.

Again, no room for panic. She may have missed her train and had to stay somewhere near Bern. She forgot her charger and her battery ran out, that was why her phone did not ring. Or maybe, she was too angry for what I had done that she decided to disappear. You never know how women think. Maybe if I gave a generous amount of money to this young receptionist, he would tell me the truth. There is a perfectly good explanation for everything that was happening. At this moment I was playing with the chances in my head. Those were the facts, and these were the options:

A. She slept in another hotel because she didn't want to travel back at night.

B. She is mad at me and she's avoiding me.

C. She's dead.

What would you think?

"It's terrible. Terrible." High-pitched, agitated voices came from the hotel lobby. I approached to hear better. Everyone was talking about the terrible incident with the train. Someone mentioned the time that the two trains collided. And then I remembered. Mary had sent me three text messages on my cellphone that I had not yet read. I took my phone out of my pocket and hesitated for a few moments before I read them.

Message number one was the confirmation that she had bought both tickets and that she would wait for me on Platform 3 in the central station of Zurich. The second message was a casual question that in the event I'm late, I should text and inform her. The third message explained "I'm a bit worried, I hope you're okay. The train started. Please call me when you see this. I can wait to get back and tell you all about my interview. Fancy for a late dinner at my hotel? Say around 9pm?"

So, she was not mad at me but worried. Her plan was not to stay in Bern, she was planning on returning. Still, you can never know what goes on in a woman's mind. Before I chose option C, and go completely paranoid, I had to learn the facts. I had to find her.

"Excuse me?" I approached people

talking about the terrible incident. All of them stopped talking and looked at me as if I had interrupted the most important conversation in the world. "I couldn't help but hear you talking about the terrible train accident. Do you happen to know how many victims were they? Or if they have announced their names yet?"

"Was there someone you know on the train?" asked a woman who was constantly looking at her cell phone, obviously waiting for some urgent news.

"No, not really. Well, actually… yes."

"They are being announced right now," screamed a man, watching the television. The receptionist turned up the volume. The air around me was cold again. My ears started buzzing, cold sweat was running again through my body, and the heartbeat on my chest felt like a big, strong hand pounding a wooden door, ready to break it down.

There were two women with the name Mary on the list of casualties. Mary Elizabeth Johnson and Mary Grey. How was

I supposed to know her last name? There was only one way to find out and it was standing right behind me.

"Hello again. Would it be possible if you could tell me Miss Mary's last name?" I looked at the receptionist with stinging, watery eyes. I could tell from the look of his face, after seeing the names that he knew. He knew that Mary was dead. It took him exactly seven seconds to reply.

"Excuse me, sir, I'm afraid I cannot share this kind of personal information."

"This is a matter of life and death. You know, right? Do you know if she's dead?"

"Sir, I'm sorry, I'm not allowed to share."

"Well, maybe this will change your mind," I rudely interrupted him and took my wallet out of my pocket. I gave him an incredibly huge amount of money. The receptionist looked at the money and then at me. He didn't say a word, and slowly put the money under the desk, while searching on the computer. It is a wonder how easily these little pieces of paper can rule someone's life – can rule an entire planet. After exactly one minute – which seemed like the longest minute of my life – he turned the screen for me. And there it was. Mary Grey.

> *"It is a curious thing, the death of a loved one. We all know that our time in this world is limited, and that eventually all of us will end up underneath some sheet, never to wake up. And yet it is always a surprise when it happens to someone we know. It is like walking up the stairs to your bedroom in the dark, and thinking there is one more stair than there is. Your foot falls down, through the air, and there is a sickly moment of dark surprise as you try and readjust the way you thought of things."* - Lemony Snicket

4

NAPOLI, ITALY

So many people were lost because of me. I wonder if I deserved it. Everyone I had met on these trips, has died. Death was chasing them. It was chasing me.

I was going crazy. I may have been since the day I was born. But am I crazy? All these accidents happened. They were not coincidences. Someone caused them. Someone killed those people. It was Death dressed as human being. Those people deserve to be remembered – they deserve my respect. I needed to find Death and defeat Him.

Up to this point, I considered myself lucky to have survived. I was just a bystander to my friends' tragic loss but not yet the victim. Maybe Life was preparing me for my own end. It was Luck that kept me alive. I could have been on any of those trains. If I went to Lyon earlier with Toma and Charline. If I had never defended old Mary, I could have taken the same train for an excursion in the city. If I had woken up in time, I would have been with Mary. But my time had not yet come.

"Signore?" An Italian voice disturbed my thoughts.

I raised my head and saw a middle-aged man with a strange black mustache. I answered in English to let him know that I am not Italian.

I had left Switzerland, still pursuing my goal, a goal that I intended to accomplish, no matter the cost. So, my fourth trip was in Italy, Milano. I chose this destination maybe because I wanted to feel a little closer to my homeland, Greece. The reason? Maybe it was a reassurance that I was close to familiar lands. Maybe that was where the confidence and courage I felt in dealing with everything came from. Or maybe it was a delusional motivation to keep me going.

"The train leaves in one minute. Are you boarding, sir?" the man asked me in English. Apparently, the ticket inspector wanted me to board on this train.

"No, no, thank you," I answered. I was not crazy enough to get on a train. What irony it would be. After all that I had been through, I was smarter than to lead myself to my own death. It would be a suicide.

I sat for three hours on this platform and watched the trains come and go, in vain. Nothing happened. Every train was on time, without any problem, without any accident, without any deaths.

So, what was the cause of the deaths of my four friends?

"But it will not succeed." I said out loud without realizing it, referring to Death.

"Excuse me?" asked a woman with a face like angel, sitting next to me.

"Sorry, I wasn't talking to you."

She smiled at me. I had no intention of talking to her. I had not the time or the mind to deal with anything other than the answer I was looking for, whatever that was.

However, what followed next was the beginning of the end.

"If you want to take this train, it would be wise to board now," she told me.

"No, I'm not taking this train."

"Ah! But the next one leaves in three hours."

"I'm not waiting for a train. But if you are, then you are the one that came early."

I laughed.

"I do not intend to take a train either."

We looked at each other, smiled, and stopped talking. I closed my black notebook. The skinny, ginger-haired woman sitting next to me asked me a question, the answer of which, would take more than just a simple sentence.

"It may seem strange to ask, but why are you waiting here all this time, if you do not want to take a train?"

"I will answer, if you tell me your own reason."

She laughed and looked away. She frowned for a few seconds then replied, "I like watching trains and observing people."

I was not convinced by her voice. Something else was happening. This woman had something strange at her look.

"Me too," I answered and just waited her reaction.

She then started questioning me about very personal things, which normally would not seem strange to me – but things change. I couldn't let the little things go. I had to be careful with everyone I met.

After almost half hour of talking, I got to know her better.

The beautiful woman claimed to be a journalist at a local newspaper. And I say beautiful because she deliberately wanted me and others to notice. Short red skirt, no leggings just her skinny, naked legs. A black shirt that seemed to have missed a few buttons and a vibrant red-colored lipstick that highlighted perfectly her white, shiny skin. She was currently writing an article about the train crashes that had happened last month around Europe. I was more suspicious than ever. I started thinking that not everything was coincidental. In a world as strange as mine, there were two specific paths in this woman's short future.

She was either going to die by a train crash, or by my own bare hands.

My excuse about sitting on a platform without boarding on any train, on the other hand, was that I was writing a novel about trains and train crashes based on these accidents. I even showed her my black notebook. I could easily pull off the lie, as my ex-wife was a writer, or at least used to be. She was thrilled with the coincidence and decided to mention me in her article. A new writer who began his virgin journey in the world of literature and the promotion of his work by a journalist of a well-known Italian newspaper – and all these details were wrapped around this dramatic story. Nevertheless, I did not mention anything about the tragic experiences I had with my friends. Didn't she already know them, anyway?

We live in the 21st century. I would have lost my mind if I thought that a supernatural power was trying to kill me or my friends. No more coincidences, no more curses. Everyone I meet dies. It was that woman, she was Death. "The human mind can reach the darkest oceans with struggle and suffer and come up to the surface refresh and alive." There is no limit to it. We, humans are capable of everything. Murders - train derailments - building explosions – everything. Am I wrong? Take a look in the past. We are in danger, everywhere. Land, sea, air!

But why me? This is something I could not understand. Maybe it was the only thing I could attribute to luck - To bad luck. There is not always logic inside the human mind. I know many people who dislike me, hate me I would say. But no. Evelyn Trussi, that was her name, was purely interested in the act of murder and not in the person itself. The fact that she didn't succeed the first time, nor the second nor the third, made her stubborn, consistent, maniac. "Psychosis is a natural response to being unable to solve problems," I read once in a book.

We exchanged numbers and I invited her for dinner the next day. She hesitated in the beginning, but she accepted, in the end.

"So, tell me a little bit about your job." I was trying to learn as much as I could about her, but at the same time, I wanted to trap her in her own lies.

"I have traveled a lot because of my job. I have gone everywhere. England, France, Spain, Switzerland…"

There it was! She kept talking, yet, she could not understand the mistakes she kept making. Another mistake that betrayed her identity. France- Spain- Switzerland. The three countries that changed radically and forever my life in the right order. Do you still think it was all just a coincidence? I knew that my enemy was smart, maybe even smarter than me. Nothing was made on purpose. I had to be careful.

"You seem very skeptical tonight. You don't speak much," Evelyn talked like she had known me for many years.

"I'm a bit stressed because of my novel. I'm trying to write a good epilogue for my story, but I just can seem to find the right conclusion. It would be amazing if I could finish, right before you publish your article. When is the deadline?" I asked. I was pushing her as much as I could. I wanted her to reveal her epilogue, my epilogue.

"I'm not sure yet, possibly at the end of this month."

The end was near, I could feel it. Somehow, I wasn't completely satisfied. I thought after I found the cause of my misery, it would all go away. But it didn't. My friends deserved my complete revenge. She was the killer. I was sure of it. Evelyn Trussi was the killer. Nothing could go wrong now. Right?

Time was passing and she wasn't making her move. All she was asking about was my life or my supposedly upcoming book, which I could not finish unless she had done her move. When would she kill me? She killed all my friends; it was my turn. I even proposed a train trip, just to see her reaction, but she refused.

When would she kill me? How? The

anticipation drove me crazy. The part that I didn't know what the next move would be. I had to act. I had to push her.

That night, I was so concentrated on my plan. If I pushed her to her limits, she would act, and I would be ready for her. It was as if I was waiting for that moment my entire life. For one last time, I had to be perfect and convincing to my role, the role of a clueless writer who had believed her – a performance of a lifetime. I was prepared for everything.

Evelyn suggested that we go for a walk after dinner and without realizing it, I led her to the train station.

"Why are we here?" she asked me strangely.

"Don't you know?" I asked laughing ironically. I kept looking her in the eyes.

"Hmm… no. You're acting strange you know. And it's a bit late and…"

It was 11pm. The last train route was in ten minutes. There was no one on the platform. It was either me or her.

It was the right time.

It was the right place.

It was the right way.

I should not underestimate her. No fast movements. She was very smart, and she had proved it to me. She worked patiently and with a schedule. She did not make hasty moves, unlike me. She knew that this anticipation and pretending was killing me more and more each minute. Maybe that was part of her plan, too.

"I know everything," I told her firmly.

"What do you mean?"

She knew very well what I meant. If I told her I knew everything, she would do it. She would reveal her secret by killing me, and then I could prove to everyone that I was right. Then, all the deaths would stop.

"It's the last chance. We are alone. There are no witnesses. The two of us… and the train. Like you always wanted it."

The sound of the train approaching was getting louder and louder.

"But I don't understand what you are telling me. You're scaring me."

I took a step towards her. She took a small step back, while standing in front of the train tracks.

"Look, I don't like what you are doing. If you want… what I think… I told you, I am engaged. There is nothing more."

"You are still acting? Is this another trick?" I asked angrily.

"What? Which trick? What are you talking about?"

"Come on. Do you actually think you could get away with something like this? France? Spain? Switzerland?"

"I don't understand anything. You're scaring me. Do not come any closer to me."

The sound of the train approaching was louder than her voice, than my thoughts. At last, I managed to silence the voices in my head for the first time. Either me or her.

I grabbed her neck with both hands. She was trying in vain to resist. She had her chance to kill me. Now it was my turn.

"Why don't you do it, damn it? Why?" I shouted at her as I squeezed my hands closer to her tiny neck. Her eyes were watering. She could barely speak. She grabbed my hands, trying to escape. Her eyes were screaming *help*, but I knew at that point that it was all a cheap performance which would end soon. The sound of the train grew louder and louder. The louder the sound, the more I squeezed her throat.

"What are you waiting for? What?" I shouted in despair.

Suddenly, a voice was heard in the distance. I could hardly hear her. A policewoman and the ticket inspector were running toward us.

My hands lost their strength and released her neck. She could hardly breathe and cry for help. I looked at her. Then looked at the train. A black, deadly, machine with blinding lights and a mysterious white smoke coming out of it, approaching us. Then I looked back at her. This is all I wanted. To push her limits. And then I did it. I pushed her.

The train had stopped, unaware of what was underneath it.

Unsuspected people disembarked from their last route safe and sound. Maybe they were going home having a hard day at work. Maybe they were returning from a visit to a friend or relative. Maybe they were looking for a place to hide because they had just committed a crime. The human mind has no logic. Whatever the reason, everyone was safe.

As for me? I was running fast, as though a raging dog was chasing me. I had done it; I had taken my revenge. But why did it feel like I hadn't?

> *"To learn to take revenge, you must first learn to suffer."* - Voltaire

5

THE LAST DESTINATION

The police are looking for me. I did not make it in the end. Death managed to defeat me. There are just a few minutes left, separating me from the end, that others decided for me.

Thirty-five years later and I still have no control of my life. I never had. What did I win? What did I experience? What did I learn?

Life choices are in vain. I do not know what else to believe. I do not know what else to think. I give up before I completely lose my mind and harm more people. Everyone died because of me. Have I started losing my mind? Have I lost it already? After committing the worst of the crimes, I can hardly say anything but the following: this book, when it is found, will show everyone the truth. Everyone will learn that life is a game that no matter what you do - whether you play or not - in the end you always lose. There are rules you must follow in order to extend the duration of the game, but there is always a game over. It either ends without warning or you just decide to finish it yourself. My pride could not let another opponent defeat me. I had to end it myself. And although it's not a move that satisfies me, it still gives me the choice, the free will.

There are other players in this game. Some of them are by your side, same team. They are willing to help you, to support you, even to break rules, to do some damage for your sake. Unfortunately, you cannot choose them all. They appear throughout the game. Sometimes they last forever and some other times they just come for a short time, long enough to change the course of it. Maybe, they are the ones who make you feel like the master of the game. They are the ones who give this game value.

On the other hand, there are opponents; the other team. They are the ones who make the game interesting. These kinds of players are willing to devour you, to destroy you without second thought. All they want is to extend the game to their advantage, even if it means they get you out of it permanently. But there is no real victory. In the end, everyone loses and leaves the game, and then they're all replaced by new players. So why do we keep playing? I guess it's what they call the illusion of victory. An illusion that remains unsatisfied and all you want is more and more.

When this book is found, everyone will know that the concept of logic does not exist. There are so many factors to consider - emotions, luck, fate, other people. Prometheus risked his life to give man fire, because only he, of all beings, possessed reason and could use it. The real question is if logic is the one and distinct thing that separates us from animals. Do we use our logic to its fullest potential? When in a situation like mine, can you think as a logical human being or will you act like a wild animal?

When my book is out, everyone will know that there is nothing accidental in life. Everything is decided by others. It is the actions of others that determine our own. There is not a single moment in your life, that its route cannot be affected because of other people's choices. Allow me to elaborate. A young man goes out to buy cigarettes from a store near his house late at night, but it's closed. He then crosses the road on his way back and a car speeds past him and injures him. Maybe kills him. Is it accidental? Who will be to blame? Will it be the young man who wasn't careful while crossing the road? Will it be the driver who was driving at high speed? Or maybe the owner that closed his store earlier that day? Or maybe it was the young man's best friend, who, a few hours ago, had taken the last two cigarettes of the pack? Or maybe it was the driver's girlfriend's fault who was arguing with him over the phone while he was driving, causing him to drive fast and carelessly. Or maybe it was the store owner's wife's fault, whose waters had broken early, causing her husband to close his business earlier and run to the hospital?

When my book is out, everyone will know that there is no justice in this life. Innocent people lose their lives every day through no fault of their own. Without having done anything wrong in their lives. Others want to lose it but cannot succeed, no matter how many times they try. While still others live a sinful life and eventually commit suicide just to escape hell. And finally, there are those who live a normal life, because they do not dare go against the law. This is the category where I belong. People who have lived a boring life, without ever having done anything bad or anything good and just wait for their meaningless life to bring them one step closer to death. They live with the illusion that their life and their existence have meaning and value. So much value, that they believe that someone is trying to kill them. They believe and imagine that innocent people lose their lives because of them.

When my book is out, everyone will know that I - my name does not matter - am currently writing the last words in this book of truth and I am on a bridge, one step before my last journey. I started with a goal: to make five journeys this summer. The first was in France and I would describe it as bittersweet. The second was in Spain and I would call it incredibly tragic. The third was in Switzerland, which I would describe as extremely short. The fourth was in Italy, and I would call it strangely random. And finally, my fifth journey can be better described as… the most beautiful…

> *"Death is worth more than a miserable life, because one stops suffering since one no longer has the feeling of misery."* - Euripides

EPILOGUE

Five days and five nights I spend looking at the ceiling, overthinking everything I have experienced. My husband, my ex-husband, the man I once loved and adored was dead. First a paranoid, then a murderer, and at last dead. You think you know someone and then life surprises you in mysterious ways.

He had changed, that was certain. He had asked me a few years back to start a family, to have our own babies. And my answer was divorce. I would never regret this life-changing decision of mine and this notebook is the proof of it.

When a man loses his job and gives up his life, he expects others to provide for him, and does not try even a little bit. When a man's sister attempts suicide, and he has become so cynical that he refuses even a visit at the hospital. When his best friend suffers from depression and his only response to that is "I hate weak people." When sorrow, despair and misery settle in, you find the strength to distance yourself and let the broke ones choose their own path.

I don't feel repentant for this. I couldn't have saved him. I could only save myself from him and that's what I did.

The bell rang. I ran to the doorstep and welcome my good friend Luck. As promised, she visited me a few days after I received the black notebook. We chatted a bit about our lives, but what I was dreading the most, was the conversation about the black notebook, about him.

She took a sip from the black coffee and said,

"When I saw the body, I was shocked. There were a few witnesses on the spot and they identified him immediately as the man who killed this poor journalist. It was so difficult for me reading that notebook and knowing that the man behind this was…"

"Luck! It's over now. It was his choice. It was his life."

"I know, but don't you wanna talk about it? I mean how do you feel?"

"Honestly? I feel relieved."

"Relieved?" My answer seemed to surprise her. It was time for me to stop hiding behind a broken, paranoid man.

"Yes. He was not well. He lost his mind after his company went bankrupt. He was jealous of my career success and he couldn't admit his failure. He never tried. And then, as you know, life happened. One thing after another pushed him over the edge. He needed just one more push."

"You sound like you wanted him to die."

"It was the only way for him to be saved. It was the only way for him to stop hurting everyone around him. I'm just glad he didn't get to ruin the lives of these people he met on these trips."

"Ellen! These people you're talking about. They're dead." Her voice trembled.

Luck was never the person who sugarcoated words. She would say what she wanted to say.

"Better than with him."

"You know… sometimes I think you start looking exactly like him. You live here all alone. You hardly ever talk to people or go out. You don't write anymore. You talked about how he gave up. But what about you? Do you want to end up like him?"

I looked at her and smiled. I preferred not to answer. I politely asked her to leave. I promised I'll keep in touch, but we both knew this was the last time we would see each other. She took the black notebook with her. She couldn't leave it here; it was evidence after all. I had made copies because I knew I wouldn't read it only once.

It seemed that both good and bad luck came into our lives, mine and his, but a little too late. First the bad, which managed to completely destroy us, and then the good. Good luck came into our lives but for him it was already too late. For me, I chose it to be late as well. After all, like he said, nothing is predetermined in life, everything is choices. And that was mine.

THE END

ACKNOWLEDGMENTS

First, I would like to mention three people in my life, without whom my love for writing and literature would have never been encouraged.

My biggest fan, my biggest supporter, and best friend, Nefeli.

My partner in life and in crime, who has never given up on me and always pushes me to be a better version of myself, my love, Andreas.

And last but not least, my inspiration and my strength for everything in this life, my brother Gregory.

No one has ever believed in me like you three and for that I am forever grateful.

To the editor, Aaron Gallagher and his exceptional work, helping me bring this work into its final draft.

To the graphic designer Konstantina Vatavali for her amazing work on the cover of this book.

To Nicolette Beebe, who has helped me with writing flaws and grammatical errors.

To Indies United Publication House, which made my dream come true.

To my family and friends who have shown me a great deal of support and love.

And, finally, I would like to thank all the readers and fellow indie authors. Your support means the world to me and I hope this story move you and inspire you.

ABOUT THE AUTHOR

E. L. Bean (Eleni Bina) comes from Greece but lives in Zurich, Switzerland with her life partner since 2018. As a fictional writer by night, and an English teacher by day, Eleni loves traveling, reading, photography, and movie nights.

At the age of ten, she discovered her passion for writing and reading, and since then, she has never stopped trying until her biggest dream come true. Through her stories, Eleni wants to make an impact on people's life and make them fall in love with the art of literature.

To find out more about the author and
connect with her, visit her webpage at:
www.indiesunited.net/el-bean

9 781644 562703